The Tyrannosaurus Game

BY Steven Kroll   ILLUSTRATED BY S.D. Schindler

MARSHALL CAVENDISH CHILDREN

Jason

Sophia

Rachel

Jasmine

Tommy

Emily

Text copyright © 2010 by Steven Kroll
Illustrations copyright © 2010 by S.D. Schindler
All rights reserved
Marshall Cavendish Corporation,
99 White Plains Road, Tarrytown, NY 10591
www.marshallcavendish.us/kids

Library of Congress Cataloging-in-Publication Data

Kroll, Steven.
The tyrannosaurus game / by Steven Kroll ;
illustrated by S.D. Schindler.

—1st ed.
p. cm.
Summary: One rainy day at school, a group
of children works together to make up a story
about their adventures with a tyrannosaurus.
ISBN 978-0-7614-5603-2
[1. Tyrannosaurus rex—Fiction. 2. Dinosaurs—Fiction.
3. Storytelling—Fiction. 4. Imagination—Fiction.]
I. Schindler, S. D., ill.
II. Title.
PZ7.K9225Ty 2010
[E]—dc22

2009005957
The illustrations are rendered in ink,
gouache, and watercolor.
Editor: Margery Cuyler
Printed in China (E)
First edition
1 3 5 6 4 2

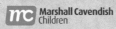 Marshall Cavendish
Children

Benjamin

Rusty

Roberto

Susan

Ava

Jimmy

So Jimmy started . . .

"Last Saturday, I was eating breakfast,
when all of a sudden a tyrannosaurus came
crashing through the window."

And Ava said . . .

"I went over to Jimmy's house, and there was a tyrannosaurus at the table. It was eating up all the eggs and making a mess."

And Susan said . . .

"I was on my way to soccer practice, and I heard a roar from Jimmy's house. I ran across the street, and Jimmy and Ava were pushing a big tyrannosaurus. Suddenly the tyrannosaurus sneezed, and we were all blown out the door."

And Roberto said . . .

"I was waiting for the bus when Jimmy and Ava and Susan and a tyrannosaurus came flying out onto the street."

And Rusty said . . .

And Benjamin said . . .

"I was on the bus, and Jimmy and Ava and Susan and Roberto and a tyrannosaurus squeezed in. Everyone started yelling!"

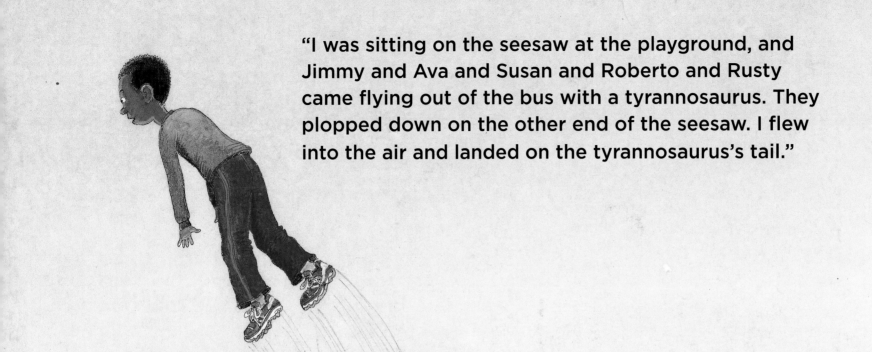

"I was sitting on the seesaw at the playground, and Jimmy and Ava and Susan and Roberto and Rusty came flying out of the bus with a tyrannosaurus. They plopped down on the other end of the seesaw. I flew into the air and landed on the tyrannosaurus's tail."

And Jasmine said . . .

"I was on a swing, and Roberto and Ava and all my friends came dashing by with a tyrannosaurus. And I jumped off and ran after them."

And Emily said . . .

"I was starting my motorbike near the playground, when out raced Ava and Benjamin and Rusty and Jimmy and Susan and Roberto and Jasmine and a tyrannosaurus. And they all jumped on behind me, and we took off for the amusement park."

And Rachel said . . .

"I was walking my dog when all the kids from school raced into the amusement park with a tyrannosaurus. I ran in after them, and my dog came too."

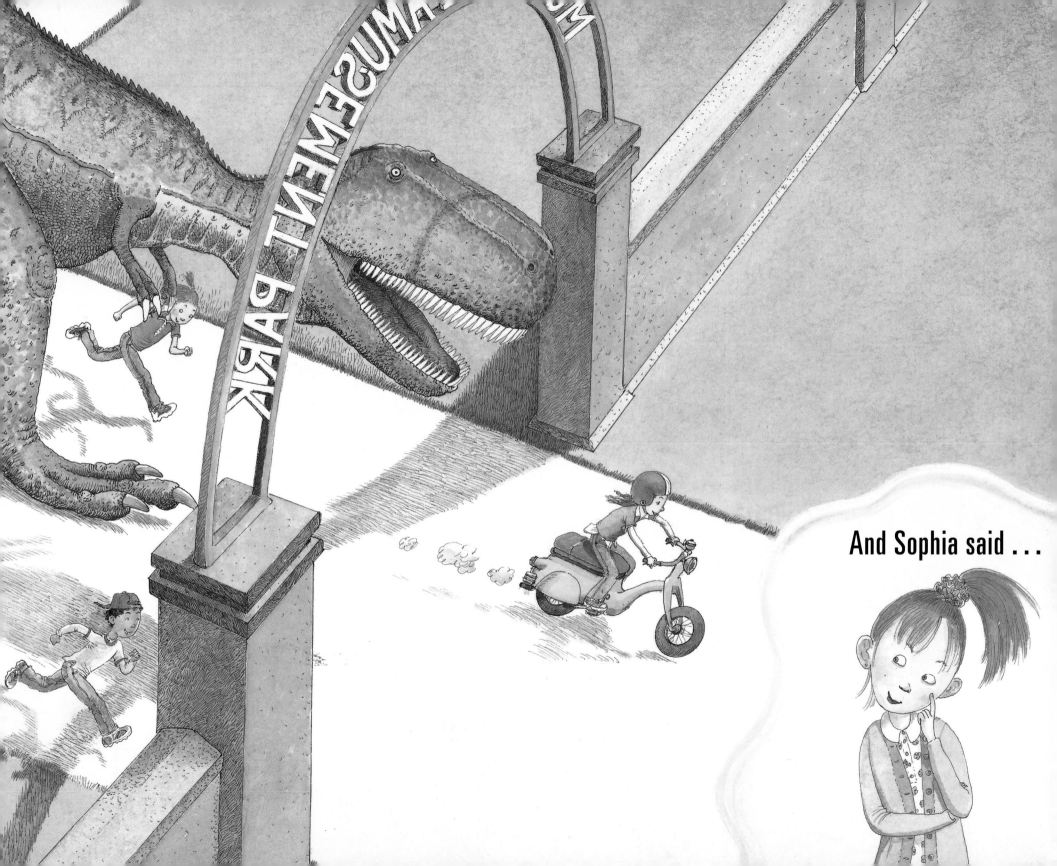

And Sophia said . . .

"I was on the roller coaster, and I turned around and there was a tyrannosaurus with Jimmy and Ava and Susan and Roberto and Rusty and Benjamin and Jasmine and Emily and Rachel and Rachel's dog."

And Tommy said . . .

"I was on the merry-go-round, and a tyrannosaurus came charging past with all my friends. It knocked over the man who takes the tickets and ran away."

And Jason said . . .

"And then the cops came and looked all over the city, but the tyrannosaurus was gone!"